MW01717438

Lil' She & Lil' Me

OUR MISSION

Lil' She & Lil' Me tells real stories about dynamic women to young girls early and often. We introduce character traits critical to a young girl's early development through childhood stories of successful women. Join our movement and give the young girl in your life a glimpse into the childhood of a strong, female role model.

TM & copyright © 2015 by Lil' She & Lil' Me
All rights reserved.
Published in the United States.

Visit us on the Web!
www.lilshelilme.com

ISBN: 978-0-9962491-0-2
Printed in the United States of America.

This book belongs to

Lil’ ________________

Lil' Pauline

creates a curious concoction

Inspired by Pauline Brown

Written by five dynamic women at Harvard Business School

Lara Avsar
Katherine Barasch
Vatsala Deora
Ariana Fahrney
Anna Khan

Illustrated by Charlotte Fassler

Lil' Pauline eagerly waited for the elevator to her grandmother's apartment. She did this every Friday afternoon. Though she was exhausted after a long day at school, Pauline was excited to see Grandma Matilde. Spending time with Grandma Matilde was one of Pauline's favorite activities.

DING!

The elevator chimed as it landed on the 13th floor. Pauline ran out quickly towards apartment 13J. "Omi, I'm here!" Pauline announced as she opened the door.

Pauline always called Grandma Matilde "Omi," a German word for grandmother. There was no answer, but Pauline knew exactly where to find Omi. She threw her backpack on the floor and ran to the balcony, where she spied a familiar, enormous purple hat.

"What are you planting today, Omi?" Pauline asked as she perched down next to her grandmother. Omi had a long line of potted plants, which included lilies, lavender, and cherry tomatoes.

"Well, my dear," Omi replied, "I had such an adventure this morning. I went to the supermarket to buy milk, and I saw these beautiful, bright daisies. I grabbed the last bunch!"

"That's wonderful!" Pauline exclaimed.

"Aren't they exquisite?" asked Omi.
"Let's plant them together so that we will
soon have our very own magnificent daisy bed!"

As they pushed the daisy stems deep into the pots, Omi told Pauline stories from her childhood.

"I loved to invent," Omi remembered. "I had so much fun creating new things. I liked sewing dresses for my dolls and making bracelets for my friends."

At 4:00 pm, Pauline remembered that she had to go to Granny Hedy's house. Granny Hedy was going to teach her how to make linzer cookies – a traditional Austrian dessert.

"Take this daisy with you," said Omi as Pauline hugged her goodbye. "Put it in a glass of water next to your bed to remember our wonderful afternoon."

Pauline skipped down the sidewalk, the daisy bobbing up and down in her backpack. Suddenly, something small and shiny caught her eye. She crouched down to find a bronze key in the grass.

"What else can I find today?" Pauline wondered.

She bent down to pluck
a handful of grass

...and a long, pale pink feather

...and a tiny little ladybug that
she placed gently on her shoulder.

Proud of her newly found treasures,
Pauline walked on, humming softly to
herself.

Just as Pauline arrived at Granny Hedy's doorstep, she heard a voice from the kitchen.

"Pauline, is that you?" Granny Hedy called. "Come on over and help me in the kitchen! I just started mixing the cookie batter. Don't forget to wash your hands and put on an apron."

Pauline watched Granny Hedy carefully measure flour, butter, and sugar.

"Granny Hedy, why can't we use all of the sugar?" Pauline asked.

Granny Hedy smiled and looked over at Pauline.

"My bubala," she said, "the magic of the recipe lies in the right mix. Never a pinch too much, and never a pinch too little."

"Now it's your turn. Add one tiny drop of vanilla to make the cookies absolutely perfect."

Just as Granny Hedy pulled the golden brown cookies from the oven, the front door opened.

"Hello! Where are my favorite bakers?" a voice called from the hall.

"Mommy, come help us sprinkle powdered sugar on the cookies!" Pauline exclaimed as she ran out to greet her mother.

At 5:30 pm, Pauline and her mother headed home. As they walked down the street, Pauline told her mother about all the little treasures she found that day.

After taking a few more steps, her mother pointed to something sparkly on the sidewalk. "Look, Pauline! Maybe you can add that to your collection."

Pauline saw a large, glittery necklace shimmering in the sunlight. She picked it up and placed it gently in her backpack next to the bottle of vanilla from Granny Hedy.

As soon as Pauline got home, she ran to her room and emptied her backpack. She lined up her treasures on the bed slowly, just like Granny Hedy did with the ingredients for the cookies.

All of a sudden, she remembered that Omi asked her to put the daisy in a glass of water. She bolted out of her room towards the kitchen but came to a halt outside her parents' bedroom. The sweet, summery scent of her mother`s perfume made her smile. The door was slightly ajar so Pauline stepped inside.

Pauline walked shyly to her mother's side and tugged on her dress.

"Mommy, please spray some perfume on me too," she said.
"I want to smell just like you!"

Pauline's mother giggled and placed the bottle on a high shelf.

"Lil' Pauline, you smell lovely just the way you are," her mother replied.
"Now isn't it time for your bath? The big family dinner is tonight."

Pauline flopped on her mother's bed with a frown on her face. She knew she could not reach the bottle, but she still really wanted some perfume.

"What should I do?" Pauline wondered.

At that moment, Pauline's grandmothers popped into her head. Pauline's eyes lit up with excitement.

"I'm going to create my own perfume!" she shouted, jumping up immediately.

Pauline rushed to find an inventing outfit. She put on her bathrobe and pretended it was a lab coat. Out of the corner of her eye, she spotted her swimming goggles.

"Aha, my science glasses!" She snapped the goggles around her eyes confidently.

Pauline looked at herself in the bathroom mirror with her hands on her hips and her head held high.

"Let the inventing begin!" she announced.

Pauline grabbed a glass and looked around for her first ingredient.

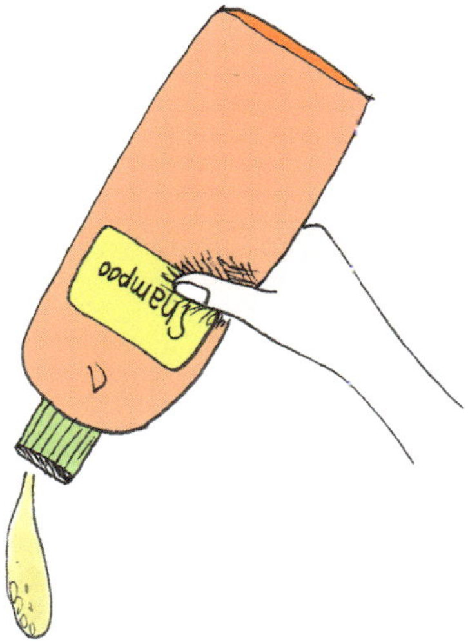

Into the glass, she squeezed a dollop of shampoo

...blended a splash of hand soap

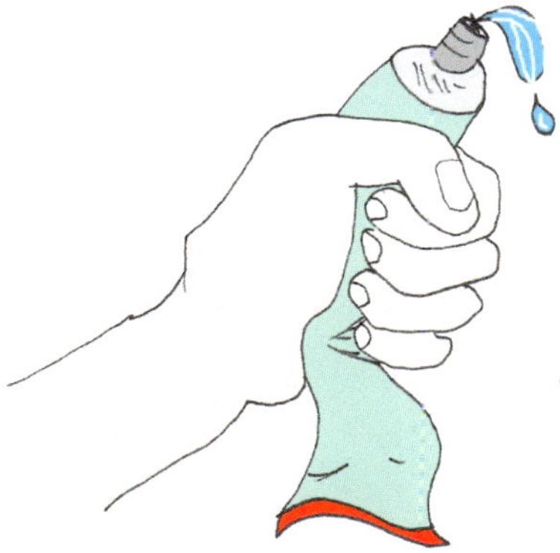

...twisted a speck of toothpaste

...and stirred a healthy dose of bubble bath to make it all fizz!

Pauline sniffed her bubbling concoction like an expert. She smelled mint from her toothpaste and roses from her shampoo.

"I need some color and sparkle," she noted as she walked slowly to her bedroom. She was careful not to spill any of her special perfume.

Pauline inspected the trinkets on her bed.

She shook the necklace over the glass and watched gleefully as swirls of pink glitter fell into the perfume.

To top it all off, Pauline dropped in her precious daisy.

The perfume reminded Pauline of a sunny spring day spent dancing between rows of flowers.

The glass twinkled, but something was missing. Pauline saw the small bottle of vanilla from Granny Hedy.

"Never a pinch too much, and never a pinch too little!" she sang as she poured one tiny drop into the glass.

Pauline's perfume looked magical. It was overflowing with pink and blue bubbles. She walked downstairs to the dining room to show off her incredible invention.

"Pauline, where have you been?" asked her mother. "What on earth is that in your hand?"

Everyone turned to look at Pauline.

Pauline stood tall and announced, "I would like to present a brand new perfume – Pauline's Perfume!"

Pauline's family clapped as they passed around the glass and tried on the perfume. A sweet and fresh aroma spread through the room.

Later that night, Omi walked Pauline back to her room.

"I'm so proud of you," said Omi. "You just invented your very first perfume! I wonder what you will think of next."

Pauline laughed and snuggled under the covers. She imagined the walk she would take tomorrow and all the new trinkets she would find. She could not wait for the start of another adventure.

The Rest of Lil' Pauline's Story

Pauline Brown is Chairman of leading luxury goods company Louis Vuitton Moët Hennessy Inc., the North American arm of LVMH Moët Hennessy Louis Vuitton SA. She provides regional leadership for nearly seventy brands in sectors including perfumes, fashion, leather goods, cosmetics, watches, and jewelry.

Pauline grew up in New York as a first generation American. Her mother, a native of South Africa, and her father, born in Austria, fostered a formal and intellectual household environment. Balancing out this proper home life was Pauline's strong sense of curiosity, to which she attributes much of her later professional success.

Pauline remembers visiting her grandmothers frequently. Grandma Matilde, whom she called Omi, lived on the thirteenth floor of an Upper East Side apartment building in New York City. Granny Hedy lived near the beach in Long Island and made spectacular linzer cookies.

Pauline graduated from Dartmouth College and later received an M.B.A. from The Wharton School of the University of Pennsylvania. She began her business career at Bain & Company and later held various positions across major luxury goods companies, including The Estee Lauder Companies. Prior to joining LVMH, Pauline was a Managing Director at private equity firm The Carlyle Group, where she invested in consumer and retail companies.

She and her husband Marshall Brown have two children, Julian (age 13) and Arianna (10), and live in New York.

Lil' Pauline had no idea that creating her first perfume would lead to a successful career in the luxury goods industry, but she was certain that her curiosity would lead to all sorts of adventure. We hope the little girl in your life stays forever curious.

CPSIA information can be obtained at www.ICGtesting.com
Printed in the USA
LVIW01n0228010515
436856LV00013B/47

9780996249102